Sita Brahmachari

Worry
Angels

With illustrations by
Jane Ray

Barrington Stoke

First published in 2017 in Great Britain by
Barrington Stoke Ltd
18 Walker Street, Edinburgh, EH3 7LP

www.barringtonstoke.co.uk

Reprinted 2018, 2019, 2020, 2021

Text © 2017 Sita Brahmachari
Illustrations © 2017 Jane Ray

A CIP catalogue record for this book is available
from the British Library upon request

ISBN: 978-1-78112-695-0

Printed in Great Britain by Ashford Colour Press Ltd

Contents

This story is dedicated to three inspirational teachers –

Miss Stowe, a sunny presence in the lives of thousands of children … and a maker of papier-mâché angels.

Maggie Barron, who taught me to follow the lines in the sand that led me to write my own stories.

Grace Emily Manning, 'Amazing Grace', a young artist with wild hair and an even wilder imagination.

Chapter 1
Broken Pot

I pull my duvet up over my head and press my hands hard against my ears, but the sound of Mum and Dad arguing still hurts.

"You promised to tell me if we couldn't pay the rent again!" Mum yells. "What are we going to live on now, sea air?"

I can't hear what Dad says, but it makes Mum get even more angry.

"You can't keep burying your head in the sand," she shouts.

Then their voices grow quiet, but quiet like the kettle's quiet on the stove, before it starts to whistle as it boils.

I wait for it ... and ...

The front door slams.

I run to my window to see Dad jump on his motorbike and speed off, turning onto the low road that curves around to the sea.

I listen to the growl of the engine till the bike vanishes along the coast road. Now there's only the sound of the waves lapping in and out, in and out. I try to make my breath slow to match the water's ebb and flow. Dad taught me to do that when I feel like this ...

slow and even
deep breaths in
and out

in with the wave
out with the wave.

Mum's in the garden below, her head slumped. The light from my window shines across her face.

"Is Dad coming back this time?" I call down to her.

"When did this garden get so wild?" she says, her voice all splintered. "Get some sleep, Amy, my lovely. Don't worry, we'll sort something out."

That's not exactly an answer, is it?

Mum goes back inside and I stay by the window, watching and waiting. The stars glitter like it *should* be a perfect night.

I look down at our garden where me and Dad planted forget-me-nots last summer. I can't see them. Is the bright blue of the flowers hidden under weeds and nettles?

I leave the window open, climb into bed, pull the duvet over my head and wait and wait and wait for the roar of the bike that means Dad's coming home ...

I knew I wasn't worrying about nothing ... I could feel this coming ages ago. And this is what happened the week after.

A man and a woman are packing boxes into two vans. There's a lorry next to the vans and two men are taking all the big things – the TV, the beds and even Mum's Welsh dresser. I can't make out their faces. Behind the road the sea crashes against the sea wall, sending spray across my face.

"Wake up! Amy, wake up!" the waves cry.

A vine spreads across our cottage covering the stone walls and draping the doorway like a curtain. Now the man and woman push the vine out of the way to get inside. They come back to check everything's gone. A girl is sitting in a huge plant pot in the corner of a room. The man and the woman come over to pick up the pot with her inside it. They pull at the girl in the pot in a tug of war. She shouts and screams at them to stop, but they're yelling so loud at each other that they can't hear her. Then they drop the pot and it breaks open. The girl's dress is made of ivy vines that spread over her body and her hair.

"You've broken the pot!" the woman screams at the man.

"No. You've broken it!" the man screams at the woman.

Then they get into their vans, one each, and drive away.

The girl is left alone in the garden, tangled in vines, picking up the pieces of her broken pot.

Chapter 2
The Cul-de-Sac

We've moved, Mum and I. Our new home is in a low-rise block of flats in a cul-de-sac. All the dirty grey walls look bumpy like they've got under-skin spots. I feel my forehead that used to be smooth. I suppose we match. Mum and me are in the 'Garden Flat'. Mum says we're lucky to get a flat at all, but I don't feel lucky.

I thought a garden flat would have a garden, but Mum says it just means it's on the ground floor. There are a few window boxes with weeds in, but that's not a garden, is it? Mum says I can keep my plant pots in the bit of ground under the windows.

"Hopefully no one will pinch them." Mum looks around, like she's not too sure.

Then she takes the key and opens the lock. The flat has been freshly painted but it still smells of someone else. Not a bad smell or a good one ... it just doesn't smell of us.

"A bit of a matchbox, but room for us two!" Mum says. "At least we don't have too much stuff."

What do I care about stuff *when Dad doesn't live with us any more?*

My room is really small, but a whole wall of it is a window. The opposite of my tiny bedroom window in Clay Cottage. When I opened the Clay Cottage window, the waves would sing me to sleep. But I don't even know if you can open this huge new window.

Mum stands on a stool to put up my old curtains. She bites her lip at the massive gap between the curtain and the sill.

"A bit half mast, but they'll do for now," she says.

They're far too short. They don't fit. Nothing fits.

The street light burns into my room. I'll never sleep. It will be like a searchlight shining on me all night.

*

Mum's friends from 'the old days' bring beer. When they first arrive they're quiet because Mum tells them I'm asleep, but when they've had a few drinks they forget. Even Mum forgets and I can hear every word.

"But you and Ned," they all say. "You two were *made* for each other!"

"That's what we thought," Mum says. "But we were so young, like school kids playing at being grown up."

"But that perfect little cottage ... and Ned was doing so well with his pottery families!"

"He stopped making them," Mum says, cutting them short. "He decided that doing the same thing over and over wasn't proper art. He'd break them on purpose."

I put an extra pillow over my head to muffle the bitter cut of Mum's voice.

Instead, I hear Dad's voice in my head. "Remember, your imagination can take you wherever you want to go."

We've walked to the top of High Moor. Dad's got one arm around me and one arm around Mum and there's a clear view down the valley. The

green unfolds in squares bordered by hedges. It reminds me of a patchwork quilt.

We lie on the grass looking up at the blue forget-me-not sky.

"Why don't we get a dog and hide up here away from the world's madness?" Dad says.

"Ever the dreamer," Mum says and she stands up. "Clay Cottage is cut off enough for me, and I don't have time to walk a dog."

Mum wanders away, and me and Dad go to look inside the broken-down cottage.

"This would be my perfect home," Dad tells me. "It just needs doing up, that's all."

At breakfast I pluck up the courage to ask Mum.

"That place where Dad's staying, it isn't broken down any more ... is it? There's electricity and heating and stuff?"

"It's not derelict," Mum says. "Someone did it up a bit after we saw it."

Then Mum's phone rings ... and she hands it to me without even saying hello.

"Here. You can ask your dad about it."

I take the phone into my bedroom.

"Hello, Amy May."

"Hi, Dad."

"How are you? How's the flat?"

"There's no garden."

"I thought it was a garden flat ..."

"They just say that to make it sound better," I tell him. "What about your cottage? Have you got electricity and heating? Is the roof fixed? Is there a place to make your pots? Is your kiln set up? Can I stay? Have you got a dog?"

"Hey! One thing at a time." Dad laughs. "When I'm settled you can come and stay – at half-term. There's electricity and water, but no heating. I'm fixing up the chimney and with a fire it'll be cosy. My kiln will soon be set up too."

"That's great, Dad. But you know how you don't want to make pottery families any more … well, I could, couldn't I? You could teach me and then we'd make some money and we can move back home again … Dad! Are you there?"

The phone is full of the noise of heavy rain and Dad panting for breath.

"I always said I wanted to feel the weather! Listen to that rain, Amy." I can hear Dad shake rain off his clothes.

"So what do you think … about the pottery families?" I ask.

"Oh, Amy, we can't go back."

I bite my lips together to stop myself from crying.

"Where are you?" I say. "Are you near that post box?"

"Yes, I can see it from here. How did you remember that?"

"When we walked past it I got one of my random pictures in my head of a sheep with an envelope in its mouth, posting a letter!"

Dad's laughing now. He sounds kind of wild, but I love to hear him so happy.

"I'm in a sheep shelter," he says. "It pongs, but it's got a signal. I can come here every day and we can talk –"

"I don't want you to be there."

"It's not that stinky!"

"I mean I don't want you to be on your own, Dad," I say. "When are you getting a dog?"

The phone goes all crackly and "rescue" is the only word I catch.

Then the signal cuts out. I go to the kitchen and hand Mum her phone. She doesn't ask me about Dad ... she just carries on unpacking.

"I don't want to go to school," I say. "I want to live with Dad."

Mum doesn't look up.

"Sorry, Amy. It's not an option." Her voice is stern. "It's way too lonely up there for you. Dad needs to sort his head out and ... it'll be good for you to go to school ... make new friends."

What about Dad? What'll be good for him?

Chapter 3
Weeds

At night, Mum lights a candle. It smells like the wood smoke in the old burner at Clay Cottage and makes me want to cry.

I curl up on the bed and shift about to get comfy. I wish I was back in my old bed.

What if Dad has an accident like the time he burned his hand in the kiln?

What if his pots keep breaking?

What if he's ill?

The thoughts whirr around my head. I can't stand it. I need to be at Clay Cottage listening to the lullaby of the sea ...

slow and even
deep breaths in
and out
in with the wave
out with the wave.

"Dig up the weeds and he'll come back, dig up the weeds and he'll come back." The words come to me as the waves swish in.

I climb down the vine that's grown in the window and drop into the nettles ... they're as tall as me. I wrap my fingers round the thick stems and tug them out. My hands sting and prickle but I keep going until one blue forget-me-not sits alone in the patch ...

The motorbike engine gets louder as Dad rides up.

"What are you doing, Amy, sitting in the nettles?"

He picks dock leaves and wipes them over my hands. Green sludge dyes my palms.

"I weeded them out, Dad. I've made it nice again."

Dad shakes his head. "You're stung all over ... even your face. I'm sorry, Amy. It's too late now ... but look at this brave blue flower."

I worry the skin on the side of my mouth with my tongue.

I look in the mirror. I've got a cold sore the size of a raspberry. It stings.

"Here, dab this cream on," Mum says, handing me a tube.

There's no way I'm starting at a new school with this on my face.

Mum looks in the mirror too. She's got a new job. "What do you think of my uniform?" she asks, pulling a face. "Is the skirt a bit big?"

I nod. It's way too big.

"Worry makes you thin," she says. "Look at you! You're a bean pole too, Amy. We need to eat more."

I lick at the cold sore and shudder.

"Tell you what." Mum takes my hand. "Let's look at the school from the outside, see how we get on."

*

The school is called Sandcastle Secondary, but there's no sea here.

We stand and stare at the metal and glass building that looks more like an art gallery than a school. The outlines of hundreds of children move like ants along the corridors.

"Once you get to know it, Amy ..." Mum starts to say.

I can tell by her voice that she knows I won't go to school today.

"I can't come here, Mum!" I say and turn away.

I won't go the next day or the day after that either.

*

Mum shows me a leaflet with a sad-eyed boy on the front. It asks –

"Is your child a school refuser?"

I shrug, go to my room and close the door.

I don't feel like a refuser.

A refuser sounds like someone who's strong and determined.

A refuser sounds like someone who doesn't go to school because they've had a good think and decided it's not for them.

I lie on my bed and listen to Mum talking to someone on the phone. She's talking about me and how I won't go to school.

"Thank you, yes. The school advised me to speak to you."

...

"We only moved three weeks ago."

...

"Her father and I have recently split up."

...

"Yes, she's always been a bit of a worrier."

...

"She was home schooled before. Her father taught her gardening, beach combing, pottery ... A big change, even without us splitting up, I know."

...

"Would that be possible? I'm working, so ..."

...

"I'll keep talking to her about school ..."

Chapter 4
Crackly Line

For the last few days, Mum's laid off me about school, but I wish she would stop sending her old friends Janine and Michelle round with 'lunch'. They hang around and try to chat and I know Mum's asked them to check up on me while she's at work.

But now it's one o'clock and I should get up.

The frosty glass in the door is sparkly with the sun and the blue of the sky shines in. A hand reaches out and knocks again.

"Who is it?" I ask.

"Mrs Nuala," a soft voice says. "From the school support service."

I have to open it.

The sun's in my eyes and all I can see is a glinting pile of silver and white plaits on top of a woman's head. They look like the ropes of a ship. Sunshine glows around her. She's wearing a long dress – the same bright blue as the sky.

"You must be Amy?"

Smile lines fan across her face like sun rays.

I nod and hover in the doorway.

"You and your mum *are* expecting me, aren't you?"

"Mum's at work," I say.

"Perhaps she didn't get the message ... about our appointment?" Mrs Nuala says, and she takes a card out of her bag. "I'll ring her again, but you keep a hold of this."

She hands me the card. Her eyes rest on my pyjamas. Then she looks past me to my closed bedroom curtains.

"You and your mum come and see me tomorrow, all right?"

Then she notices my stacks of empty plant pots.

"You like gardening? Me too," she says. "We'll fill these pots of yours in no time."

I watch the blue of her dress blend with sky and vanish into a dot in the sun. Then I read the card.

On the front is a drawing of two hands – one holding the other. On the back it says –

Grace Nuala
Counsellor
Sandcastle School Support Centre

*

I lie in bed and wait for Dad's call.

The line's all crackly again. I can only just hear him over the din of the rain. It seems like every time we speak it's raining. I think of Dad with his lanky legs scrunched up in a stinky sheep shelter and I feel sad. And the last few times he's called his voice is so flat that it seems like he's run out of things to say to me.

"Sorry, Amy ... You can get out of the habit of speaking," he tells me at last.

"Is the kiln fired up yet?" I shout over the crackle.

This huge bluster of wind drowns out his answer and the next thing I hear is –

"Oh, this is impossible. I'll write, Amy. Will you write back?" He's shouting now. "I'll write, I promise ..."

The line goes dead.

In my head I hold Dad's hand and walk up the hill with him in the rain. I don't think it was his dream to live at the top of that hill, lonely and wet, all on his own.

*

After work Mum comes and sits on my bed.

"Did you hear from Dad?"

"Yes, but the signal's so bad ... He says he'll write."

Mum bites her lip.

"How was your work?" I ask her.

"There was this baby born today ... Even smaller than you were, Amy. Her skin so clear and thin. She made me think of you when you were born."

"Oh, Mum!" I shudder. "Don't go on about that again."

Mum hugs me into her chest, like I'm still a baby even though I'm nearly up to her chin now. But I don't mind. If she could see under my skin she would know how much I need a hug. She holds me close and kisses the top of my head.

"The school support service called," she says into my hair. "The lady said you've already met. Seems like there was a bit of a muddle ... We'll see her tomorrow."

'Anything's better than being on my own, sleeping away the day,' I think.

"All right," I say.

I sense Mum's surprise that I don't put up more of a fight. She gives me one last squeeze and goes to make the tea.

I close my eyes to block the glare of the street light.

slow and even
deep breaths in
and out
in with the wave
out with the wave.

And after hundreds of waves ...

A blue dress and a yellow sun spin towards me.

Chapter 5
The Art-House

The Sandcastle Support Centre is an ordinary brick house that looks like all the others in the street. There's a green metal gate and a front garden full of straggly flowers, growing over cane arches.

Mum rings the bell and Mrs Nuala comes to the door. She has on a yellow dress, the exact same style as her blue one. Perhaps she sews her own. Her hair is loose today – it's really curly and so long that it reaches all down her back. She grabs a handful of it ...

"I meant to tie this lot up!" she says. "But anyway ... you can find us how we are. Not very tidy!" She laughs and lets go of her tangly hair. "Come on into my art-house. Excuse me, I'm just finishing a call."

We're in a room with a huge table in the middle, stacked up with art work, bits of cloth, tubes of paint, jam jars with dirty water and piles of old shoe boxes. A sofa is crammed into the big window that looks on to the front garden. The walls are covered in drawings and paintings ... some of them by children, some by adults. There's a book shelf that dips in the middle because it's stacked so full. There's picture books for little ones and some for grown-ups, like the graphic novels I used to read with Dad. At the far end of the room is a big glass conservatory that's a bit like our ramshackle greenhouse at Clay Cottage. A vine grows up the windows, tiny bunches of purply

grapes hang down. The doors are flung open onto the garden.

"It's an art-house all right. Looks like our messy classroom at Clay Cottage!" I whisper.

"That's just what I was thinking." Mum grins.

Inside the conservatory is a big sandpit with cushions around the edges. We walk around it and have just stepped out into the garden when Mrs Nuala comes to finds us.

"See what I mean, Amy. There's plenty here to fill those pots of yours. You'll help me tame this garden, won't you?" She beams at me, then turns to Mum. "Call me Grace," she says. "You too, Amy. It's good to see you here."

Mrs Nuala – Grace – sits on the cushions next to the sandpit. Mum and I do the same.

"But isn't this place for primary school kids?" I ask, as I look at the pictures and the sandpit, at the objects and toys.

"It's for everyone. Primary, secondary, parents ... pensioners like me!" Grace taps her chest.

"You're not a pensioner," Mum says.

"You know what they say!" She smooths her hands over her face. "Black don't crack ..."

I must be scowling because Grace wags her finger at me. "And, Amy, brown's not supposed to frown!"

She laughs, but I think about the deep frown lines on Dad's face.

"Is that true?" I ask.

"Oh Amy," Grace says. "It's just my joke. Worry lines are more about what people deal with in their lives than their skin colour or their age. But I *am* ready to retire. You'll be my last little group of students this term. It's going to be special!"

Little group of students – that's all it takes to set me off.

Dad used to tell me not to worry about the future ... but no one gets the way my mind works. The things I can't see and the people I haven't met yet – those are the exact things I worry about the most.

Grace scoops up some sand ... and lets it run through her fingers.

"So, Amy? Are you happy to come to school here for a bit – till you feel more ready for Sandcastle Secondary?"

"OK." I nod.

"Can I stay too, instead of going to work?" Mum jokes.

But Grace doesn't laugh. "This is a family centre. When Amy's settled, you can come along sometimes, see how she is." Grace takes Mum's hand and I see tears well up in Mum's eyes.

"Why don't we all sit down?" Grace touches Mum's arm and we sit at the table. I bump into a big metal bin as I tuck my legs under.

"Why's this bin full of newspaper?" I ask.

"If ever you're short of anything to do you can always rip up some news for me," Grace says. "It's for my papier mâché."

"What's papier mâché?" I ask.

"Mashed paper – of course! I use it to make angels."

"Angels?" I say. I can't think what an angel made of mashed paper could be like.

"Now, where is he?" Grace looks in a few boxes stacked up near the sandpit. "Ah here ..." She takes out a model of a little boy with wings on his back. "This one got left behind ... I call these my worry angels. I make them for you children when you're ready for school."

"Will you make one of me too?" I say, holding my hands out to look at the angel-boy more closely.

"Do you want me to?" Grace asks.

I nod as I run my fingers over the angel's papery wings.

*

"What's your favourite cake?" Grace asks.

"Chocolate!"

We look up a recipe and write a shopping list. Grace gives me a cloth bag full of coins.

"I need to get rid of all this change," she says as we walk up the road together. "I'll wait outside ... I've got to keep an eye out for the other family."

The other family.

A vine of worry tangles up my chest – it's growing into me.

I find chocolate, flour, butter and eggs and lift the bag of change onto the counter. The old man behind the till laughs.

"Is that you, Gracie?" he calls out, as he peers around the door.

"How did you guess? This is Amy ... my new student. Amy meet Lester ... my old friend!"

"Less of the old!" Lester grins.

I empty a pile of coins out and look up at the man's twinkly eyes.

"Take your time, no rush."

I count out the money and pay him £5.62.

"Good job," he says. "I love a till full of change!"

On the walk back, Grace tells me about the family who are coming to see us.

I like how she says "us" as if we've known each other for ages instead of this being my first day.

"The girl who's coming to our art-house has just arrived here. She's from Syria. Have you heard about the war in Syria?"

"I've seen the news," I tell Grace.

"Well then, you'll know it's been a long, hard journey for that family. The girl's name is Rima and she's lived in a refugee camp for a year. She's your age, Amy, and it's our job to welcome her. You'll help me, won't you?"

*

I can hear Grace on the phone. She sounds annoyed.

I get on with the cake in the kitchen. I measure out what I need and follow the recipe all on my own.

"Two hours!" I hear Grace say. "That's not enough. I need a translator *all* day. What am I supposed to do for the rest of the day? ... God knows what the family's endured ... It's fine if the translator is a volunteer as long as she can be with us all day, every day ... OK. I'll expect them tomorrow."

By the time Grace hangs up, the cake's out of the oven, I've cleaned the kitchen and am colouring in a tree in a doodle book. I've got about thirty different shades of green on the table.

Grace looks at my doodle tree. "Beautiful," she says. "Come on ... let's find some real trees!" Then Grace stops and sniffs the air. She points to the cake and says –

"So that's what smells so good. Shall we sit in the sun and eat cake?"

There's something I need to know. "The girl who's coming tomorrow?" I say. "What's her name again?"

"Rima."

"Rima," I say. "Maybe we should keep the cake for Rima."

Chapter 6
Fragile

At the end of the day, I'm waiting for Mum to pick me up. The doorbell rings.

"Answer the door to your mum," Grace says. "You can practise on her."

"*Ahlan wa sahlan*," I say.

"What?" Mum asks with a grin.

"It means 'welcome'!"

Mum looks from me to Grace as if she wants us to explain.

No one does, so she walks in anyway.

"Have you been gardening?" she asks, as she takes my hand and looks at the mud under my nails.

"Gardening and all sorts!" Grace sits at the table and fills in a form. Every time she reads out a subject she says "tick", does a huge tick in the air and flings her arms about in a dramatic way.

Maths – tick
Food and Nutrition – tick
English – tick
Art – tick
Biology – tick
Science – tick
Languages – tick

When she's done, she hands the form to Mum and the phone rings again.

"Sorry – I have to get this. Don't forget your bulbs, Amy!" Grace points to the bags by the door and waves us off. I hand Mum the plants Grace gave me and I pick up the big tub of compost.

"You *have* been busy," Mum says as we leave. "What have you there?"

"Not sure," I say. "Grace says they'll come up next spring."

On our walk back to the flat Mum asks me about my day and I realise that Grace wasn't making it up when she ticked those subjects off. We have done it all. The maths when I shopped and cooked … then gardening and art, the Latin names of the flowers Grace told me, and the Arabic words we looked up.

"What about English?" Mum asks as she opens the door of our flat.

"For English," I say, "we read this poem by a Muslim poet called Rumi – because a new girl is starting tomorrow. She's a refugee from the war in Syria."

"Grace didn't tell me that," Mum says. "What was it about – the poem?"

"Worry," I say. "It went something like – Let go of your worries, and make your heart ... clear ... like when you look in a mirror and you see what's there ..."

"Tricky." Mum sighs. "But it doesn't sound like an English lesson, does it?"

I don't know why Mum's being so weird with me, like there's something wrong with the poem.

"Well, that's what we did." I shrug. "Grace says Rumi was a really great poet – like Shakespeare but in way more olden times."

But Mum's not listening any more. Instead, she bends down and picks up a postcard off the mat. She looks at the picture of sheep ambling around on a hill and hands it to me. I can tell from her face that she's not happy, but how can she can be grumpy with Dad for sending me a

card? Especially when I heard her moan
to Janine the other day how Dad has cut
himself off from us.

"You've got to really want to escape the
world to live on High Moor," Mum said to
Janine. "He must have wanted to get as far
away from us as he could."

That "us" whirrs and whirrs in my mind.
Before I thought Mum and Dad had stopped
loving each other but now I think ... maybe
Dad wanted to get away from me too.

*

I'm taking my muddy trainers off when
there's a knock at the door. A delivery man
hands Mum a package.

"Sign here!" the man says and hands
her the package. Red and white 'Fragile'
labels are stuck all over it.

We find the scissors and cut the cardboard. What's inside the box isn't that big but it's heavy and covered in bubble wrap.

It's a pottery sheep. It's wearing a beaten up old leather jacket and has a letter in its mouth to post into a red post box!

It makes me laugh.

Even Mum smiles, a sad smile but still a smile ... then she starts popping all the little bubbles. I watch her fingers, pop, pop, pop at the bubble wrap and I feel the vine of worries that I mostly forgot about today tangle up inside me again. So I read the card.

Dear Amy

I hope your new school is OK.

Today I fixed up the chimney. Things are getting sorted. I'm going for lots of long walks and putting up shelves in my workshop / living room … and yes … the kiln is all set up! The first thing I've fired in it belongs to you.

I've made friends with the taxi driver who drove me here on my first day. His name's Malik and he's sorted me out with a few things. He even gave me a sofa bed he didn't need. For you to sleep on when you come and stay at half-term.

I miss you, my Amy May.
Enjoy your pottery sheep!
Dad X

I pretend to Mum that I have to go outside and pot the plants from Grace tonight or they might die. I keep my head low so she can't see me water the pots with my tears.

Chapter 7
Welcome
ahlan wa sahlan

The next morning, Grace asks me to go into the garden and choose some flowers to brighten up the place, which is funny because I've never been anywhere brighter than Grace's art-house. I cut six orange roses and put them in a tall vase.

Grace keeps going to and from the window to look for "our visitors".

"Here they are," she cries. "Remember … our welcome?"

She flings the door open, nods at me, counts to three and we say "*ahlan wa sahlan*" together. The people on the step smile but look surprised. Maybe we didn't say our greeting right. Anyway, the tall man in a thick coat and scarf reaches out and shakes Grace's hand.

"Good morning," he says. "Thank you for this welcome."

As Grace talks to him I look past him and this is what I see.

Two boys cling onto a mum. The boys are identical – like twins – except one of them has a leg in plaster up to his knee. To the side of them are two girls, one about my age and an older girl – maybe about twenty? – who's wearing a denim jacket and a red skirt with a bold picture of a woman's face on it.

The mum and dad step to the side so the girls can come in.

"Hi, I'm Iman," the older girl says. "I'm the volunteer translator."

Grace smiles and takes both Iman's hands in hers.

"Thank you. You will be much needed," she says.

"And this is Rima," Iman says, a huge smile on her face. "Mr and Mrs Alam." She points to the twin boys. "And Ali and Asraf."

"Happy to be here," Mr Alam says in slow, clear English, but he doesn't look very happy.

Rima doesn't look up.

"And what about Ali and Asraf? How old are they? Will they come too?" Grace asks.

"They are nearly four," Mr Alam says. "They will come later. Not now."

Mr Alam doesn't look like someone you could argue with. I think how little the boys are, they don't look as old as four.

"All your family is welcome here." Grace touches Mrs Alam's arm, as Iman translates.

Mrs Alam smiles at Grace. "Thank you, thank you."

"No thanks needed," Grace says. She shows them into the living room and we all sit down.

Mrs Alam looks round like she's inspecting everything, object by object. She holds the twins on her lap as they try to wriggle away from her.

Iman translates.

"Mrs Alam says ... Thank you for your welcome. The twins cannot come now. Ali must have an operation on his leg and the twins don't like to be apart," Iman says.

I watch Iman. I've never seen anyone translate before. It's strange how much you can understand between the words ... all the things that are said with the eyes and the hands, and some things that aren't translated at all like the little noises people make when they aren't sure about something or the pause before they answer a question.

I think of all the things Mum and Dad never said to me before they split, and I wonder if one day I would make a good translator.

"Amy's made us a cake," Grace says. "Would you like to try it?"

I cut a slice of cake for each for us and Grace hands it out.

"Amy baked this for you yesterday … she's only just joined me too," she tells Rima.

Rima eats the cake politely. Then she looks up at me and her eyes glimmer with the hint of a smile.

Ali and Asraf squidge the cake and shove it into their mouths. Their mum talks quickly to them and I work out that she's telling them off for being greedy.

Mr Alam shakes his head as he talks to Iman. She translates …

"Sorry, the boys' manners are not good. They haven't had cake for so long … and it will take time for them to learn again that they won't starve."

Mrs Alam bends her head to the orange roses, breathes in the smell, then kisses Rima on the cheek. Iman translates what she says next.

"It's a long time since we have been anywhere that smells so sweet."

I keep trying to smile at Rima, and I think she's trying to smile at me, but her face doesn't move. It looks like she's forgotten how to smile. The way she looks reminds me of Dad.

Sometimes even if he was close to you he felt like he'd gone somewhere so far away that you couldn't find him.

After the cake Grace wants to speak to Iman and the family on their own, so I sit at the art table and make a card for my dad.

*

This is the card I make. I draw this room and the garden. I want Dad to see what Grace's art-house is. Even if he can't be here with me I can give him a picture, can't I? Maybe it will make him feel as if he's not so far away.

I don't *try* to listen in, but it's hard not to. Every now and then I look up to swill my paint brush and catch Rima's eye – the door into Grace's office is open. Iman and Grace talk and the parents speak too, but I haven't heard Rima's voice much yet. When Iman asks her things in Arabic, Rima's answers are only a few words.

*

Dear Dad

I love the pottery sheep. Is it you posting me a letter? Please keep making things, Dad.

I've drawn you the school where I am for now. My teacher here says I have "anxiety". Anxiety is when you really, really worry about stuff – just like you told me I shouldn't do all the time. She thinks it was too much for me to go to a new secondary, in a new city … after all the changes. I call this school Grace's art-house. Grace is my teacher.

Mum's started work at the hospital. I think she likes it.

The flat's OK. I help in the garden at Grace's art-house and she gave me some plants for the pots on the window sills and by the front door. As Grace would say, they'll brighten up the place a bit.

Plus I baked a chocolate cake. It tasted yummy. When I visit, I'll make a cake for you too.

Love you, Dad.
Amy XXX

P.S. I know how to say "welcome" in Arabic! It's "*ahlan wa sahlan*".

Love you again.
Amy May X

Chapter 8
Ripped Up News

The next morning, Mum wants to come with me to Grace's art-house to talk to her.

"What about?" I ask.

"Just checking the plan for when you'll start secondary school."

"But Grace already said … after half-term … we'll go for an hour at a time and build up."

"Still, I'd like a quick word," Mum says and she knocks on the door.

*

I take a book off the shelf and sit at the art table. The book's pale brown – the colour of paper stained with tea … and there's no words. The pictures are amazing, like giant birds floating on tiny boats carrying their giant eggs. It's like they've flown in from my dreams.

Then I sit in the sun and mess around building stuff in the sand. I draw lines in the sand, too, the way me and Dad used to on the beach at Whitby. I flatten and scrape out paths between my sand houses. Today I build Clay Cottage by the sea … the garden and the workshop.

I open the lids of some of the shoe boxes around the sandpit … and inside are masses of random little things.

Tiny boats, feathers, little doll's house people, fruit, buttons, nuts, shells, acorns, wool, cotton, dried leaves, jewels. There's even a mini motorbike. I take some tiny pots out of one box and put them in Dad's workshop – blue flowers and vines for our forget-me-not patch. Then I make waves for the sea and I find some of those little fish that curl up or down on the palm of your hand depending on how you feel. The fish tails all curl up. That means I'm feeling lonely.

It's weird how when I'm building things and placing objects in the sand, waves of memories flow into my head and the old noises too, like the angry rev of Dad's bike on the night he left, the screech of Mum and Dad as they lashed out at each other.

Mum has finished talking to Grace. She comes to say goodbye and stares at the sandpit.

"Is that Clay Cottage?" she asks.

*

"Of course," Mum says to Grace as she leaves. "I just wanted to make sure Rima's ... story doesn't make Amy worry any more ..."

"I understand, Tanya," Grace says, "but you can trust me with this."

Just then the bell goes. It's Rima and her family, and Iman.

Grace's voice changes as she introduces Mum to everyone. I can hear Iman translating.

I like how her voice joins the stream of theirs.

*

Iman's really nice. She's 23 years old and wants to work as a translator, but she's finished university and needs some real-life experience. Which is why she's a volunteer translator here with us. She wears her head covered like Rima and her mum, but her clothes are different. Today she's wearing skinny jeans, purple Converse and an arty T-shirt with a black and white drawing of a bird holding a green branch in its beak.

At first Grace tries to work with me and Rima at different times, but it's a disaster. Rima doesn't talk or do anything with Grace or Iman. Sometimes she looks in the picture books and takes objects out of the shoe boxes and peers at them, but if Iman or Grace ask her what she's looking at she just stops looking.

*

Dear Dad

I want to tell you about someone I've met at Grace's art-house. I want her to be my friend, but she doesn't speak English. She's called Rima, and she's from Syria. She's got twin brothers. One of them – Ali – had his leg crushed and he needs an operation. Rima's quiet and doesn't speak much but she's got a translator called Iman who's teaching me some Arabic.

I know your phone reception up there is rubbish, but when you can look this up. I like how the letters look on the page, like a painting.

Love you
Amy May X

*

The one thing Rima does do is rip up newspaper for the papier mâché dustbin. She's been doing that for days now.

Today there's a big photo on the front page of children on a boat in the Mediterranean. Rima starts crying and ripping up the newspaper in a frenzy. She keeps ripping and ripping, shredding the paper, and she's talking to Iman in her language. I can hear by how Iman talks that she's trying to calm Rima down, but it's not working. Rima is in such a state that Grace takes them both into her office and closes the door.

I pick up the torn paper and try to listen to Iman, but it's Rima I hear. I've never heard her speak so much – and Iman has to translate fast.

"Rima says …" Iman says, "she feels guilty because she is alive and safe and she doesn't know what's happened to her friends or her family. And she says she doesn't want people to see her only as a refugee … she wants people to see who she is … like Amy."

Chapter 9
A Penny for Your Thoughts

Grace has blown up little balloons to make the bodies of her angels. She puts on some music and we all sit around slopping glue onto the balloons to stick the newspaper on.

"Why are there four balloons?" I ask.

"Because the twins – and Mrs Alam – will be here from tomorrow," Grace says.

Iman translates into Arabic for Rima and, for the first time, Rima smiles into my eyes.

*

When Mrs Alam arrives with the twins, Grace sets her up on the sewing machine. That's where she spends most days, sewing together Grace's jumble of patchwork pieces, putting in zips and buttons, making stuff …

And now Rima seems a bit happier. She holds the twins and cuddles them. It's easier for everyone with the twins around.

We play together in the sand and it doesn't feel childish. The pictures the twins make in the sand aren't childish. Their sandcastles and sculptures (that's what Grace calls them) are of tanks, fire and guns. They find model people in the boxes and lie them on the ground, or bury them under the sand. They make different sounds for bombs and guns … and Iman doesn't need to translate those sounds. Sometimes they hit themselves and Grace gently pulls their hands away to remind them not to get lost in their memories. It's clear those memories aren't somewhere anyone should stay for long.

Sometimes Asraf holds Ali in his arms and rocks him.

One day, Mrs Alam leaves her sewing machine and sits beside the twins and holds them on her knee.

"It was Asraf who carried Ali from danger," Rima explains to me and Grace.

I can't remember if it's that day when me and Rima start to talk. It happens so slowly, a few words here and there.

I think what happens is, we play with the twins and Iman translates a few words that me and Rima want to say to each other ... and we use all Grace's little objects.

It's Grace's idea for me to build Clay Cottage again to show Rima where I used to live. And so I build our picture –

I tear up bits of newspaper to show Dad's cracked apart, broken pottery families in the bin.

I find a little plastic man in a box and put him on the edge of the sandpit. That's Dad – he walks in patchwork fields, all alone.

I make the green fields and say nothing, but Rima says something to Iman …

"Rima wants to tell you a story from her home," Iman says. "Maybe it will help you, Amy."

She pauses before she goes on. "There was a man and he had two pots – he used them to carry water from the well …"

Mrs Alam puts her fabric next to the cotton reels and scissors and sits with us. Ali sits on her knee and Asraf on Grace's knee. I've never seen them so still and quiet. They listen to Rima tell the story.

This is the story.

"There was a man," Iman translates, "and he had only two pots to carry water in. One of them was whole. The other had a crack in it. It was a long way to walk to the well and a long way to walk back. The man cursed the cracked and leaky pot because by the time he got home it was always half empty and he didn't have enough water for his plants. Anger grew and grew inside him and he decided to break the pot. 'What use is this to me?' he said.

"Then a wise woman came with her seeds and planted them all along the path where the man walked every day to and from the well. And every day, water leaked from the cracked pot ... And every day flowers grew from the seeds the woman had planted along the path, and fruit trees blossomed too. And soon everyone had one cracked pot and one whole one ... one to water your own crops and one to water flowers along the path for everyone."

"Feel about it!" Rima says when Iman finishes.

She says this a lot these days.

"*Think* about it ..." Iman starts to correct her.

"Don't correct her," Grace tells Iman. "It's great that she's speaking in English. Just let her."

Then Grace wipes her eyes with the hanky she keeps in her pocket and tears roll down Mrs Alam's face. They hug each other. The twins wriggle free and start to mess up my sand picture.

Actually, I think, "feel about it" is what Rima means.

*

Mum's new habit is to turn up early to pick me up.

She has a cup of mint tea with Grace and Mrs Alam and with Iman's help they talk to one another. When we leave, Mum squeezes Mrs Alam's hand as if to tell her "be strong".

"Why didn't you want me to be friends with Rima?" I ask Mum.

"I did. I was just worried in case you ... Oh, no matter! The fact is, I've never seen you more cheerful," Mum tells me as we walk home.

I try to explain things to Mum.

If someone doesn't speak the same language as you ... when you want them to understand not just the words you say, but what you feel, then you try to speak in any way you can ... with your hands, with your eyes, with pictures in the sand ... You act things out ... you let the feeling show in your whole body ... whatever way you can to show them you want to be their friend.

Then Mum squeezes my hand, the same way she squeezes Mrs Alam's hand ... in a way that says "I understand".

No words are needed.

Mum knows because she's here with me, together, but how can I explain this to Dad? So, that night, I write him a letter.

*

Dear Dad

I think one of the best ways to learn a language is to get a sandpit and have millions of little things to play with, like Grace has in her shoe boxes. It's like making tiny worlds. That's how Rima learns English. And I learn Arabic! Iman reckons I'm quite good at Arabic. That's because I hear Rima and her family talk all the time. But when Rima and I talk when we make sand pictures together – that's the best!

These are the Arabic words I know. I can say them – I learn them when Rima builds sand pictures, or when I sit at the table to draw or write ... And Iman showed me how to write them.

Home – sakan
Country – balad
Safety – manjāh
War – ḥarb
Love – widād but I think I've heard Rima say "habibi"
Family – bayt
School – madrasa

Sheep-Post me!
Habibi Dad!
Amy XXX

*

Grace always listens to how Iman translates and she watches how Rima and her brothers say things, what they do with their hands … the gestures they make. She's made the papier mâché angels and now she's painting them. It's incredible how she makes them look so like us when she paints in the faces.

"How many angels have you made?" I ask her.

"I don't know – hundreds, maybe more." Grace laughs. "I've got my funny ways with them. I never paint the wings till you're ready to fly!"

Grace has put a bunch of forget-me-nots in the hand of my angel. That's because I told her about our patch of garden in Clay Cottage. She lets me paint them blue and put the yellow sun dots in the middle.

I'm a good watcher and Rima is too ... so we watch and listen and I think about what Rima talks about and I think she does the same with me.

Grace has made up this game she calls "A penny for your thoughts!" We use her cloth bag of change to play.

The game is that Iman keeps count of every time we tell the others what we're thinking. Then Grace puts 10p into her bag of thoughts. At the moment the score is ...

Rima – £2.20
Ali (about to have his operation) – £15
Asraf – £6
Amy – £1

I've got good at finding out about everyone else's thoughts, but the total score of MY thoughts is the smallest.

So – when Grace says, "A penny for your thoughts!" – I say, "I'm sad that Mum and Dad split up, and I worry about my dad, but at least we don't live in a war zone with bombs and guns and tanks in our street."

Iman asks Grace if she can translate this to Rima and she does.

Grace says "comparing" doesn't help to sort your own life out – it just makes you worry about stuff that doesn't matter – but I know I compare all the time, and I bet Rima does too.

The twins and Rima have shown me loads about their lives before – in Syria. A lot of it feels like what you see on the news. But when I watch the twins move their hands in the sand, trying to make a new house for their family, it looks a bit like the pictures I build in the sand too. It makes you realise we're not that different. When I sit with Rima I understand that most of the things we want to build in the sand are the same.

Chapter 10
Angels

Grace tells me she's worried I'm too focused on Rima and her family and I've forgotten about myself. I tell Grace that I'm happy to forget about myself and she says that's fine sometimes, but not all the time.

So we have this day when the focus is on me to make or draw or garden, and talk. At first I feel stupid talking about our move from Clay Cottage, when Rima had to flee from another country where her home's been blown to bits, but Grace says, "Go on." Then I realise that Iman's translating because Rima wants to know about me as much as I want to know about her.

If you have a friend and you don't share much of the same language you have to put spaces between things when you talk to each other. Like if you want someone to understand your words you have to wait for the translator to catch up and your friend to take in what you mean.

I like that space where you can rest. I think if I could have that space with everyone, no matter what language they speak, where I have time to read people's body language and the look in their eyes, and time to take in their words, then I wouldn't worry so much.

*

At the end of the day, when Mum, Grace and Mrs Alam talk and Iman translates, me and Rima are on our own. We take everything out of the sandpit and put it away in the boxes and then smooth over the sand. When it's flat Rima opens her hand and I see two tiny figures in her palm. She hands one to me.

"Me." She smiles and points for me to place the figure in the sand.

"You," she says and places the other figure in the sand next to me.

"*Habibi* sister," I say.

It makes Rima laugh. She says the word again without sounding the "H" like I did.

"Yes!" She laughs. "*Habibi* sister."

Mrs Alam comes and sits with us. She touches Rima's head and mine and says something in Arabic. I wish I could understand.

Iman listens and then thinks hard before she translates. "It's tricky," she says, "but it's something like ... We need more than one language to show how we feel."

Grace stands by the door, a smile on her face just like the smile on Mrs Alam's face.

"Time to make angels," she says.

*

Grace has finished our worry angels. On the last day before half-term she hands us each a decorated shoe box. She says to open them when we get home.

I sit on my bed, open the box and take out a figure. She looks like me only she has wings and a dress the exact bright blue of the forget-me-not flowers in her hand. When I show it to Mum her eyes fill with tears.

"How did she catch that look of yours?"

"What look?" I ask.

"Half looking at you, half far away in dream-time." Mum kisses me on the cheek. "It's turned out good at Grace's art-house ..."

I nod, but I can't believe how fast the weeks have gone. Mum says I should leave my worry angel at home when I go to stay with Dad.

"It looks like it could break easily," she says, but I want to keep her with me.

"When you drop me off, you won't argue with Dad, will you?" I ask.

"Of course not," Mum jokes. "There'll be no time!"

Chapter 11

Trust

I watch the orange, red and gold leaves smudge past like paint colours as they run into each other. Golden rays shoot between autumn leaves. I close my eyes.

"Come on, Amy." Mum touches my arm as the train slows down.

I rub my eyes and see the outline shape of Dad standing on the platform with a shaggy grey dog.

"You brought the sunshine, Amy May!" Dad calls and steps out of the sun dazzle so I can see him now, and feel his long arms draw me into a big hug.

"You look well ... stubbly, but well," Mum says, and she points at Dad's unshaven chin.

"You too," Dad says and strokes the dog's head. "Meet Sable!"

"You know what they say about dogs and their owners!" Mum says, her voice jokey. "She looks just like you – all she needs is the old biker jacket. I like that sheep you made for Amy," Mum adds, not joking now.

I can tell she's making a big effort to make this OK for me.

I bend down to pat Sable, but she hides behind Dad's legs.

"It's OK, Sable." Dad comforts her, then turns to me and says, "She's a rescue dog – she's had a rough time. We've got to earn her trust."

*

Dad's friend Malik gives us a lift in his taxi to where the road ends. We get out and walk with Sable along the track to the top of the hill. Sable seems less stressed when she's not on the lead and she lets me run by her side. It feels good to run free amid the soft purple heather where there are no buildings or people or roads, just me and Dad and Sable.

The cottage is so snug. There are only two rooms, plus a loo. It reminds me of Clay Cottage with its low ceiling and stone floors. Dad shows me into the living room / pottery workshop with a kitchen bit at one end.

Dad lights the open fire and, as it catches, he piles more logs on. I look at everything he's made. There are owls, hawks, badgers, foxes, a horse and a sheep. He's laid them all out on little beds of heather he's collected from the moor. When I look close I see it's not just purple, but greens and golds too.

"I put the heather there so that they fit in the landscape," Dad explains. "I want the colours of the pottery glaze to blend in with my first season here. I'm making what I see around me."

"Are you going to stay here then, Dad?" I come right out with it.

"I am."

He seems so sure I don't ask him again.

Dad boils some milk and we sit by the fire with cups of hot chocolate. He wants to know what I've been doing so I tell him about Grace's art-house and I show him my worry angel ...

He's interested in how Grace made it and how she's captured the exact look on my face. While he's turning it over in his hands, it feels like the perfect time to tell him Rima's story about the two pots – the broken one and the whole one. I've waited to be by his side to tell him ...

I start like Iman did – "There was a man" – and I try to remember all the details.

Dad falls silent when I finish and we sit in that close, silent space together that most people don't feel comfortable with. It's what I love about Dad. He's never minded that space.

After a long time, Dad says, "You've made a true friend there."

*

The half-term week goes too fast.

I'm on a mission to get Sable to trust me and so I spend hours with her every day. We walk, we eat, we drink hot chocolate. I make Dad Grace's chocolate cake and I can't stop eating ... cake and big bowls of pasta, soup and anything else that me and Dad cook. I haven't wanted to eat for so long. We light the fire and we play games with Sable. Dad works a lot too. He says, "I'm feeling the clay now, Amy. I'm on a roll," and I am glad.

I sit with him and stick my hands in the cool clay. It feels heavy and dense – calm – and I hear Rima's voice in my head telling me to "feel about it". I make a plant pot for her and the blue glaze comes out perfect.

On the last night Malik invites us for a meal with his family. We're going to sleep over at their house to get Sable used to staying with Malik when Dad takes me back home.

I dip my naan in the tandoori chicken sauce. It's delicious, but I feel sad. Sable does, too. She's all hang-head at my feet as if she knows I'm leaving soon.

"I'm not the only one who will miss you," Dad says as Sable nuzzles into me when we leave her at Malik's house in the morning.

As we get in Malik's taxi, the sound of Sable's whine is so sad and high that it seems to cut me in half.

Chapter 12
Old Friends

Dad walks me to Grace's art-house. I can't wait to see Rima but I'm like Sable – all jumpy with nerves. The holiday is over and now we have to spend time in school. Grace gets to the door before we ring the bell.

"Meet my dad," I tell her as I lean in to hug her.

"Miss Seeker?" Dad asks, peering at Grace.

"I haven't been Miss Seeker for a very long time." Grace laughs. "I'm Grace Nuala now!"

"What are the odds?" Dad laughs too. "I'm Ned," he says. "You helped me after my mum died. That was many years ago now."

"How old were you?" Grace asks.

"Six," Dad says. "I look a bit different now!"

"We all do!" Grace tips my chin up and looks at Dad. "But I can see echoes of your little boy face in your Amy."

*

In the end, school was OK. People were fine. The teachers were kind. Rima and me together, we did OK, but that one hour felt like a whole day. It was good to come back to the sand.

"Step by step, one hour more each day …
And if it gets too much you can always come
here," Grace says.

"But what about when you retire?" I ask.

"Then Iman will be here and you can see
her." Grace smiles at me.

I feel glad that she's got it all worked out.

*

At the end of the day, I tidy up the sandpit and
I think of Dad and Sable. It makes me feel so
sad to think about Dad when he was a little boy
missing his mum, trying to live without her. He
never talks about her. 'What was she like?' I
wonder.

Then I think about Sable. Dad will have
picked her up by now. She'll jump up at him, so
happy to have him home. She'll cheer Dad up,
and that cheers me up too.

I see the little boy worry angel left in the sand where Ali has played with him. I pick it up to put away.

"Will your dad collect you today?" Grace asks, with a look at her watch. Mum's late. I shake my head. "I can't get over it," she goes on. "Me – your dad's teacher when he was so little, and now you. What a compliment that he remembered me!"

That's when I have the idea to ask Grace if I can give the little boy worry angel to Dad.

Chapter 13
After Grace

Rima loves the blue pot I made her. She wants
to plant an orange rose like the ones in the
art-house garden. She says those roses are "the
smell of welcome". She puts words together
like that. They don't quite make sense, but you
know what she means more than if they did –
the way Rima talks makes me "feel about" what
she says.

My pots are full of spring flowers now. I
didn't know what I was planting in the autumn,

but good things have come up. Purple tulips, crocuses and sweet little daffodils. Some bright blue flowers, too. I thought they were forget-me-nots, but it turns out they're something called "scillas". I've never grown them before.

Dad's sent me a photo to show how he's hung his worry angel above his table. He says he doesn't know what Grace puts into them, but it can't be just mashed-up old news. He thinks the worry angel is helping him with his pottery.

He's made a clay model of Sable and it's genius. Her messy, shaggy grey coat looks real and he's captured that wary look in her eyes, like she wants to trust you but she's not sure if she can yet. Everyone who's seen it wants Dad to make a model of their dogs too. I can see why. I don't know how Dad's got so many feelings into the cold, heavy clay. He's brought it to life. He jokes that the worry angel's flown into his new home with a bit of Miss Seeker's kindness … just like the kindness she gave him when he was a lost little boy.

Me and Rima are in the same class at school. We're OK, but it's so big and noisy that we get tired. Rima's learning English fast, but it's tricky for her to understand everything. She has to focus so hard. I'm all right first thing in the morning, but then I feel like I'm vanishing into this massive worry-echo that booms along the corridors like a bomb exploding in my head.

Grace has retired now, and so it's Iman who says that whenever school gets too much, me and Rima can go back to the art-house. These days, we mostly cope with school in the morning and see Iman in the afternoon. Iman works at the art-house full-time with another woman who is raising money to keep Grace's old art-house alive. Rima's mum goes there a lot with the twins. She sews curtains and tablecloths, seat covers and all sorts for their new flat.

*

"Not to enter!" Rima has come to our flat and she's leaning against my bedroom door. She won't let me in. I know Mum's in there too.

"Mum, can I get in my room please?" I shout.

"Hang on ... won't be a minute!" Mum calls out.

At last Mum opens the door a crack, peeps out and closes the door again.

"Is ready?" Rima asks her.

"Ready!" Mum says. She sneaks past my door so I still can't see in my room, then walks into the kitchen.

Rima flings the door open. At last.

"Wow," I gasp.

The most stunning patchwork quilt is spread over my bed. It's all different shades of blue – sky, sea, Grace's dress, forget-me-nots, scillas, the hijab Rima has on today. And I've got new curtains too!

"I say to my mama ... favourite colour of Amy is blue! Quilt and curtains too," Rima says, beaming with pride. "All match!"

I draw one curtain back and Rima draws the other. Then we close them again.

Rima claps her hands and swishes the curtains to and fro like a fabulous dance.

"Smooth!" she says, and she pulls me into a hug. "I will say to Mama her sewing is good. It is a very good closing and opening for us."

Rima's worry poem –

LET GO OF YOUR WORRIES

*Let go of your worries and be
completely clear-hearted,*

*like the face of a mirror that
contains no images.*

*When empty of forms, all forms
are contained within it.*

*No face would be ashamed to be
so clear.*

RUMI

Our books are tested
for children and young people by
children and young people.

Thanks to everyone who consulted on
a manuscript for their time and effort in
helping us to make our books better
for our readers.